Where Have the Unicorns Gone?

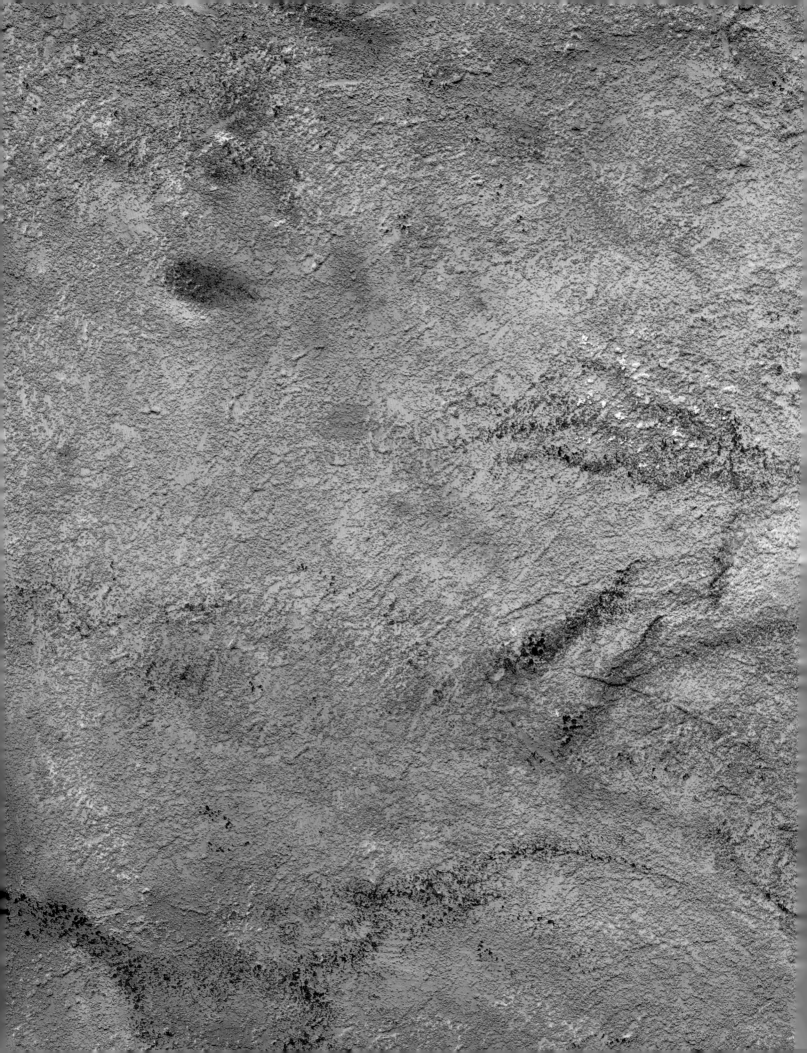

Where Have the Unicorns Gone?

BY Jane Yolen

ILLUSTRATED BY
Ruth Sanderson

Simon & Schuster Books for Young Readers

New York   London   Toronto   Sydney   Singapore

SIMON & SCHUSTER BOOKS FOR YOUNG READERS. An imprint of Simon & Schuster Children's Publishing Division, 1230 Avenue of the Americas, New York, New York 10020. Text copyright © 2000 by Jane Yolen. Illustrations copyright © 2000 by Ruth Sanderson. All rights reserved including the right of reproduction in whole or in part in any form. SIMON & SCHUSTER BOOKS FOR YOUNG READERS is a trademark of Simon & Schuster. Book design by Anahid Hamparian. The text of this book is set in 22-point Lapidary. Printed in Hong Kong 10 9 8 7 6 5 4 3 2 1 Library of Congress Cataloging-in-Publication Data Yolen, Jane. Where have the unicorns gone? / by Jane Yolen ; illustrations by Ruth Sanderson. — 1st ed.   p.   cm. Summary: The unicorns flee from the noise, violence, and destruction of civilization and find refuge in the sea. ISBN 0-689-82465-3 [1. Unicorns Fiction. 2. Environmental protection Fiction. 3. Stories in rhyme.] I. Sanderson, Ruth, ill. II. Title. PZ8.3.Y76Wh 2000 [E]—de21 99-31291 CIP

ARTIST'S NOTE

This book is painted in oils on gessoed Masonite panels. For some pages, I created a textured surface using pumice gel and modeling paste, sponges, palette knives, and sandpaper. The first layer of paint is thin and transparent. Backgrounds are painted first, then the foreground and any people or animals. It takes about two or three layers of paint for each illustration. Details are painted last.

For Bob and Ionia, with much unicorn love
—J.Y.

For Jane
—R.S.

Where have the unicorns gone?

They have left their haven of greening bowers,
Of dapple-down trees and yellow-eyed flowers,
Their dimity dells and golding glades

Where shadows shift in silver shades.

They have followed the path where the nightingale calls

Down, down to the water that tumbles and falls

To splash in the silent drifts of pool.

Where have the unicorns gone?

Routed by gouts of iron-red flames,

By helmeted knights and their steel-weapon games,

They have galloped past castles of towering stone,
Gouged from the hillsides from which birds have flown,
Past iron-plowed fields, past grazed-over ground,

They have galloped away, never looking around,

To wade in the perfect peace of ponds.

Where have the unicorns gone?

Startled by turns of the clacketing mills

Echoing hard through the catacombed hills,

And the chuggering trains on the long, dark miles,

And the sawing of trees and the stacking in piles,

And the cataphonetics of city and town,

They have fled the noise going down, down, down

To the rambling, tumbling streams.

Where have the unicorns gone?

They have scattered far from the noxious smog,

Wrapping themselves in wee wisplets of fog;

Leaving the iron-sharp city-straight scapes,

Fleeing in greying and tattered moon capes,

Away from the scenting of fire and fume,

Away from the odor of spillage and gloom,

Down to the ribbon-rolled river.

Where have the unicorns gone?

They have bounded beneath the webbings of wires,

The contrails of rockets and other steel fliers.

Silken and swift and silver and streak,

They galloped through yesterday, into next week.

They have all disappeared to the back of beyond

And into the flowering moment of dawn.

Down and away, to the endless sea.

Will we ever see them again?

If you go at night, when the moon is full,

When the waves and tide exert a pull;

If you bury your toes in the shadowy sand

And cast your eyes away from the land,

In the moment that separates nighttime and dawn,
The instant of daydream that's here and then gone,
You might see the toss of a mane or a horn
And the wavery shape of escaped unicorn

In that watery eden, the sea.

Author's Note

In all the old myths, the unicorn had an affinity for water. When a unicorn dipped its horn in a pond poisoned by toads, snakes, or basilisks, the pond immediately cleared.

Unicorns have been mentioned in the Bible, in travelers' diaries of the Middle Ages, in bestiaries, in poetry, stories, songs. They have been portrayed in books, in broadsides, in tapestries, in paintings, in movies. But was there ever really any such creature? In Lewis Carroll's *Through the Looking-Glass,* the Unicorn says to Alice, "If you believe in me, I'll believe in you. Is that a bargain?"

Perhaps it is.